Heritage Turkeys as Pets

Heritage Turkeys

Complete Owner's Guide

Including information on purchasing, raising and caring for
Heritage Turkeys as well as habitat, feeding, health
problems and breeding, all included.

ISBN 978-0-9923922-4-6

Printed in Australia

Disclaimer

Although the author and publisher have made every effort to ensure that the information in this book was correct at press time, the author and publisher do not assume and hereby disclaim any liability to any party for any loss, injury, damage or disruption caused by errors or omissions, whether such errors or omissions result from negligence, accident, non-functional websites, or any other cause. Any advice or strategy contained herein may not be suitable for every individual.

Foreword

In this book you will find the answers to all of your questions regarding heritage turkeys. Here you will find tips for raising, feeding and caring for your turkeys in addition to information about breeding, health problems and more. By the end of this book you will be an expert on the heritage turkey!

Acknowledgements

I would like to extend my sincerest thanks to my friends and family who supported me throughout this journey. I'd like to thank my wife, especially, for her endless love and understanding.

Table of Contents

Chapter One: Introduction...1

   Useful Terms to Know...3

Chapter Two: Understanding Heritage Turkeys..................5

   1.) What Are Heritage Turkeys?...............................6

   2.) Facts About Heritage Turkeys 8

      Summary of Facts...9

   3.) History of Heritage Turkeys.............................10

   4.) Varieties of Heritage Turkeys 13

      a.) Jersey Buff 14

      b.) Black...15

      c.) Narragansett 17

      d.) Slate...19

      e.) Standard Bronze...20

      f.) White Holland..21

Chapter Three: What to Know Before You Buy..................23

   1.) Do You Need a License? 24

      a.) Licensing in the U.S. 24

      b.) Licensing in the U.K. 25

   2.) How Many Should You Buy?............................27

   3.) Can Heritage Turkeys Be Kept with Other Pets?.......28

   4.) Ease and Cost of Care....................................30

a.) Initial Costs 30

b.) Monthly Costs 34

5.) Pros and Cons of Heritage Turkeys 38

Chapter Four: Purchasing Heritage Turkeys 40

1.) Where to Buy Heritage Turkeys 41

a.) Buying in the U.S. 41

b.) Buying in the U.K. 42

2.) How to Select a Healthy Heritage Turkey 43

3.) Heritage Turkeys as Food 45

a.) Benefits of Heritage Turkeys 45

b.) Tips for Buying Heritage Turkey 46

c.) Heritage Turkey Recipes 47

Chapter Five: Caring for Heritage Turkeys 53

1.) Habitat Requirements 54

a.) Space Requirements 54

b.) Building Materials 55

c.) Selecting the Right Fencing 57

d.) Maintenance Tips 58

e.) Summary of Facts 58

2.) Feeding Heritage Turkeys 60

a.) Nutritional Needs 60

b.) How Much to Feed 62

c.) Types of Food 63

d.) Summary of Facts 64

3.) Farming Heritage Turkeys 65

Chapter Six: Breeding Heritage Turkeys 67

1.) Basic Breeding Info 68

2.) The Breeding Process 71

3.) Raising the Babies 74

a.) Incubating the Eggs 75

b.) Raising the Chicks 76

Summary of Facts...78

Chapter Seven: Keeping Heritage Turkeys Healthy...........80

1.) Common Health Problems 81

2.) Preventing Illness..92

Chapter Eight: Heritage Turkeys Care Sheet 94

1.) Basic Information 95

2.) Habitat Set-Up Information...95

3.) Care and Feeding Tips 96

4.) Breeding Information 96

Chapter Nine: Frequently Asked Questions 98

Chapter Ten: Relevant Websites 103

1.) Food for Heritage Turkeys 104

2.) Care for Heritage Turkeys 106

3.) Health Info for Heritage Turkeys 108

4.) General Info for Heritage Turkeys 110

5.) Breeding Heritage Turkeys 112

Index..114

Photo Credits 121

References...125

Chapter One: Introduction

When you think of a turkey, do you imagine a big, double-breasted bird covered head to toe in vibrant feathers? This is the standard image of an industry-bred turkey, but it is a far cry from what natural, heritage turkeys look like. In 1784, Benjamin Franklin actually suggested that the turkey become the national bird of the United States. If Franklin could have seen the way the food industry has changed his beloved bird into a genetically-modified food product, he might have changed his mind.

Heritage turkeys are not only a popular food source and alternative to genetically-modified poultry, but they are also becoming more popular as pets. These rare birds were once near extinction, with only about 1,300 accounted for in the United States in 1997. Just nine years later, in 2006, a turkey census revealed that the population had soared to nearly 9,000. This number continues to grow as more and more people realize the value of these animals as pets.

In this book you will learn everything there is to know about heritage turkeys. In addition to learning basic information about these birds, you will also receive a variety of interesting facts on what they are and how they became popular as pets. You will receive answers to all of your questions regarding how to raise and care for heritage turkeys, including information on breeding them and raising the young. By the end of this book, you will be an expert on the heritage turkey.

Useful Terms to Know

APA – American Poultry Association

Aviculture – the scientific study of birds

Banding – a form of identification, putting a tag or band on the wing or leg of a bird

Beak – the protruding mouth part of a bird, typically divided into an upper and lower part

Bedding – the material scattered on the floor of a pen or enclosure to absorb moisture

Brood – to care for a batch of chicks

Chick – a baby bird

Clutch – a group of eggs laid at one time by a single female

Coop – a cage or enclosure in which birds are housed

Flock – a group of birds living together

Hatch – the process through which a chicken comes out of the egg

Hen – a female turkey

Incubate – to keep eggs at a certain heat and humidity, allowing the embryos to develop properly

Molt – part of a female bird's reproductive cycle during which she loses her body feathers

Pinfeathers – a new, developing feather on a bird

Poult – a young domestic turkey, chicken, pheasant or fowl

Shank – the part of a bird's leg between the foot and hock

Tom – a male turkey

Wattle – the flap of skin under the chin of a turkey or chicken

Chapter Two: Understanding Heritage Turkeys

Before you can decide whether a heritage turkey is the right pet for you and your family, you need to learn everything there is to know about them. Though heritage turkeys are still fairly rare compared to industry-bred turkeys, they can make wonderful pets if you know how to take care of them. In this chapter you will learn the basics about these turkeys including what they are, some interesting facts about them and their history as pets. You will also learn a few facts about the different breeds of heritage turkey. By the end of this chapter you will be ready to move on to learning some of the specifics about keeping these birds as pets.

1.) *What Are Heritage Turkeys?*

The name heritage turkey is given to a variety of strains of domestic turkey which retain their historic characteristics. While the majority of the turkeys raised for food in the U.S. have been genetically modified, pumped full of antibiotics to increase their growth rate, heritage turkeys are similar to wild turkeys and to the turkeys that were bred naturally for food during the 1800s and early 1900s.

<u>In order to qualify as a heritage turkey, the breed must meet three criteria</u>:

- It must mate naturally – industry-bred turkeys are often made to reproduce through artificial insemination (its genetic line must also have been bred naturally)
- It must be able to live outdoors and experience a long and productive life – these birds can roost, run and fly, unlike many industry-bred birds
- It should have a slow growth rate – up to 28 weeks, compared to the 12-week growth span of industry-bred turkeys

As mentioned earlier, the heritage turkey is not a particular species or even one strain of turkey – it is a name given to several different breeds of domestic turkey. There are about ten different breeds which meet the qualifications to be named heritage turkeys. These breeds include:

Auburn	Royal Palm
Jersey Buff	Slate
Black	Standard Bronze
Bourbon Red	Midget White
Narragansett	White Holland

Though heritage turkeys have been increasing in popularity, they are still rare in comparison to industry-bred turkeys. Heritage turkeys are raised at an annual rate of about 25,000 compared to over 200 million industry-bred turkeys. In some aspects, heritage turkeys can even be considered endangered.

2.) Facts About Heritage Turkeys

While heritage turkeys are primarily raised as a food source, they can also be kept as pets. These turkeys range in size and color depending on their breed, and many of them are very attractive. Unlike commercially-bred turkeys, heritage breeds are meant to be hardy and self-reliant – they should be able to live outdoors and to eat a natural diet. They mature more slowly than commercial breeds, but they do not experience as many health problems because they aren't pumped full of antibiotics and growth hormones.

As it has already been mentioned, heritage turkeys are not a certain species but a group of domestic turkey breeds. The scientific name for the domestic turkey is *Meleagris gollapavo*, the name for the birds which descended from wild turkeys and were first domesticated over 2,000 years ago. Heritage turkeys tend to live longer than commercially-bred specimens, having an average lifespan of 5 to 7 years. In many cases, however, males (called toms) live only 3 to 5 years.

These turkeys range in size and color depending on their species. For the most part, however, females range in size from 12 to 16 lbs. (5.4 to 7.25 kg) and males range from 20 to

28 lbs. (9 to 12.7 kg). Heritage turkeys display a wide range of colors from all white to a pattern of black, white, brown and tan. Most breeds have a hard pink or black beak with a red or blueish head and a pink or red wattle beneath the chin. The tail color varies by breed.

Summary of Facts

Scientific Name: *Meleagris gollapavo*
Breed Information: ten different breeds
Lifespan: 5 to 7 years average
Development Rate: market ready at 28 weeks
Qualifications: naturally mating, long productive outdoor lifespan, slow growth rate
Size (female): 12 to 16 lbs. (5.4 to 7.25 kg)
Size (male): 20 to 28 lbs. (9 to 12.7 kg)
Color: varies by species: white, brown, tan, slate, black, buff
Characteristics: hard pink or black beak, red or blueish head, pink or red wattle

3.) History of Heritage Turkeys

For several centuries, North American turkeys were raised on small family farms to provide families with meat. These turkeys were raised on a natural diet and were often used as a form of pest control – they tend to eat a variety of insects in addition to grains. As factory farming became the standard of food production, however, turkeys came to be bred selectively – only the largest specimens were chosen for breeding.

From the 1920s to the 1950s, nearly all other types of turkey were replaced by the production of broad-breasted fowl. Large, broad-breasted birds were favored because they had more breast meat and thus would fetch a higher price. During the first half of the 20th century, the Broad Breasted Bronze, developed from the Standard Bronze, was the breed of choice. By the 1960s however, turkeys came to be bred even more selectively – breeds that did not show dark pin feathers were favored and thus the Broad Breasted White turkey came to dominate the industry.

As demand for turkey increased, producers ramped up their production and sought to increase their profit margins by finding ways to produce the maximum amount of breast meat at the lowest cost possible. To do so, the single most important trait in turkeys bred for food became breast size – in most industry-bred birds, the breast accounts for nearly 70% of the total weight of the bird. This being the case, turkeys bred for meat became so heavy and unbalanced that they were incapable of walking or breeding normally. To solve this problem, producers began to use methods of artificial insemination to keep up with the rising demand for turkey.

1 - Bourbon Red Turkey

As the demand for broad-breasted turkeys grew, other breeds began to fade into obscurity. In fact, by the end of the 20th century nearly all but the Broad Breasted White breed of turkey were in danger of extinction. In 1997, the American Livestock Breeders Conservancy identified the heritage turkey as one of the most critically endangered of all domestic animals. Upon taking a census, the conservancy found that fewer than 1,500 breeding birds existed in all of the United States. Some breeds had fewer than 12 individuals left.

As awareness grew in regard to the plight of the heritage turkey, several groups of poultry enthusiasts sought to restore the breeding population. The Livestock Conservancy worked with Slow Food USA, the Heritage Turkey Foundation and the Society for the Preservation of Poultry Antiquities to increase the breeding of heritage turkeys.

Within a few short years, a new census revealed that the population of heritage turkeys had risen by more than 200%. By 2006, the number of breeding heritage turkeys was around 8,800 birds. Though certain breeds like the Royal Palm and Bourbon Red are still considered critically endangered, heritage turkeys as a whole have been making a comeback.

4.) *Varieties of Heritage Turkeys*

Because there are specific criteria which a breed must meet in order to be considered a heritage turkey, the numbers are limited. There are, however, ten breeds which have been identified as heritage turkeys. These breeds include:

Auburn	Royal Palm
Jersey Buff	Slate
Black	Standard Bronze
Bourbon Red	Midget White
Narragansett	White Holland

Unfortunately, many of these breeds are still rare and their numbers continue to dwindle. The Narragansett is the oldest breed of heritage turkey and, in 2002, a census revealed that there were only a few hundred specimens of the breed left. Royal Palm and Bourbon Red turkeys continue to struggle – they are all but extinct.

For a description of several popular heritage turkey breeds, see the following list:

a.) Jersey Buff

Also referred to simply as the Buff, the Jersey Buff turkey is named for the color of its feathers. Though this breed never became as widespread as some other heritage turkey breeds, it was officially recognized by the American Poultry Association in 1874. During the late 1800s, production of the Bourbon Red variety increased, which led to a decline in numbers for Buff turkeys. By the early 1900s they had become quite rare.

The greatest advantage Buff turkeys had for processing was the fact that their pinfeathers were white. It was very difficult, however, to breed birds to meet the color standard which is another reason the breed suffered. The Buff color standard calls for an even buff coloration throughout the bird with lighter flight feathers. In 1915, the Buff turkey was removed from the American Poultry Association's Standard of Perfection and, as a result, it became nearly extinct.

In the 1940s, however, interest in the breed was renewed and the New Jersey Agricultural Experiment Station initiated a breeding program. The program was designed to produce a small to medium-sized market turkey and the result was the modern Jersey Buff. These birds were developed through crosses with Black, Bourbon Red and

Broad Breasted Bronze birds. The modern Jersey Buff has reddish-buff colored feathers with a white tail having a light buff-colored bar near the end.

Young males of the breed weigh about 21 pounds (9.5 kg) and mature hens about 12 pounds (5.4 kg). Hens of the breed have been known to be good egg producers. This breed is particularly recommended for small scale or hobby farms due to its calm disposition and the fact that it is easy to work with.

b.) Black

The Black turkey is one of the few heritage turkey breeds that did not originate in North America. This breed is a direct descendant of Mexican turkeys that were transported to Europe by explorers during the 1500s. This breed became particularly popular in Spain where they were known as Black Spanish turkeys. In England, they were particularly popular in the Norfolk region, gaining the nickname Norfolk Blacks.

The Black Spanish turkey made the trip back to the Americas with early European colonists and it was soon crossed with wild turkeys. This crossing formed the foundation for the modern Black turkey breed in the United States. Though not as popular as the Bronze, Black turkeys were bred in large numbers along the eastern coast of the U.S. in Virginia and Maryland. This breed was particularly popular for its calm disposition and rapid growth rate.

2 - Spanish Black Turkeys

The Black turkey gets its name from its lustrous black plumage. Many specimens of the breed exhibit a dull black under color with a greenish sheen on top of the feathers. Any brown or bronze cast is considered undesirable in the breed. The beak of these birds is black and the wattle red, though it may change to blueish-white. The skin of these turkeys is typically white, though it may have a yellowish tinge not seen in other heritage breeds.

The standard weight for a Black turkey is about 23 pounds (10.4 kg) for young males and 14 pounds (6.3 kg) for young hens. This makes the Black turkey slightly smaller, on average, than the Standard Bronze. This breed was recognized by the American Poultry Association in 1874 and, because it hasn't been selected for production attributes in recent years, many modern specimens of the breed may actually be smaller than the breed standard.

c.) Narragansett

This breed of turkey gets its name from Narragansett Bay in Rhode Island, where the breed was originally developed. Narragansett turkeys are descendant from the turkeys brought over to America by English and European colonists starting in the 1600s. Most likely developed from Norfolk Blacks, these turkeys eventually became the foundation of the turkey industry in New England. They were popular throughout the country, but their primary market was in Connecticut and Rhode Island.

An account written in 1872 stated that a breeder flock of a dozen hens could produce flocks of one to two hundred Narragansett turkeys. These birds required little supplementary food, feeding primarily on insects like crickets and grasshoppers. The breed was recognized by the American Poultry Association in 1874 and the standard for the breed came to include young males weighing between 22 and 28 pounds (10 to 12.7 kg) with females weighing 12 to 16 pounds (5.4 to 7.25 kg) at maturity.

Though it was once the foundation of the turkey industry in New England, the popularity of the Narragansett breed began to decline in the 1900s. This decline was a direct result of the increase in popularity of the Standard Bronze. It wasn't until the early 21st century that interest in the breed was renewed, based on the biological fitness and superior flavor of the breed. Modern interest in this breed continues to grow and it is becoming a market niche.

The Narragansett turkey's color pattern includes black, gray, white and tan. The pattern itself is similar to that of the Bronze, though steel gray or black replaces the coppery bronze of the latter breed. A genetic mutation results in white wing bars that remove the traditional bronze coloration – this particularly coloration is not known outside the United States. These birds have a horn-colored beak with a black beard and red or blueish head. The feet and shanks of the bird are salmon-colored.

d.) Slate

Some people suggest that the Slate turkey originated from a cross of the Black turkey with a white turkey, but there is little evidence to confirm this. Rather, evidence suggests that the gene for slate coloration is a legitimate mutation, similar to the unique blue coloration in the Andalusian chicken. It is also true that there are actually two genetic mutations which combine to produce a blue, slate-like color. One of these mutations is dominant and the other recessive – this results in different shades of slate.

The Slate turkey gets its name from its blue, slate-like color. Though the exact shade may vary, the color is typically an ashy blue with or without some flecks of black. Some other names used to refer to this breed include the Blue or Lavender turkey. These birds have a horn-colored beak with a red to blueish-white head, throat and wattle. Females of the breed are usually lighter in color than the males. Males also tend to be heavier, weighing around 23 pounds (10.4 kg) while females are about 14 pounds (6.35 kg).

e.) Standard Bronze

The Standard Bronze, also referred to simply as the Bronze, has long been the most popular type of turkey in the United States. This breed originated from a cross between wild turkeys in North America and the domestic turkeys brought over by European colonists. This cross resulted in a bird that was tamer than wild turkeys but larger than the European birds. Bronze turkeys are named for their coppery-bronze coloration, a color inherited from their wild ancestors.

Though this type of turkey existed during the 1700s, it wasn't until the 1830s that they were given the name Bronze. The Bronze turkey was actually recognized by the American Poultry Association in 1874 after their breeding had been standardized. Since this time, the status of the breed has changed. Crosses with broad-breasted birds from Europe resulted in a larger, faster-growing breed that came to be known as the Broad Breasted Bronze. This breed eventually came to be the primary commercial variety of choice in the U.S.

Unfortunately, due to commercial breeding, the Standard Bronze has largely been left behind. It wasn't until the 21st century that interest in the breed was renewed and a niche market was created. Today, the Standard Brønze is known for having a stately appearance. Males of the breed average around 25 pounds (11.3 kg) while females mature at about 16 pounds (7.25 kg).

f.) White Holland

Throughout American history, the White Holland turkey has been the most important white-feathered breed. Today, however, the White Holland is one of the rarest breeds and also the most difficult to authenticate. During the first half of the 1900s, the White Holland was the only all-white commercial variety. Its main advantage was the fact that it lacked dark pinfeathers – this gave it an edge over other breeds, even though they were not as large.

What gives the White Holland its unique coloration is actually the result of a mutation. White turkeys have been bred selectively for centuries, all the way back to the Aztecs. It is possible that white turkeys were brought to the Americas by Dutch settlers or European immigrants, though there is no documentation to support this idea. By the 1800s, however, the White Holland was popular in the show ring in the United States and it was recognized by the American Poultry Association in 1874.

The White Holland is decidedly showier in appearance than other heritage breeds. It has snow white feathers with a red to blueish head. The beard is black and the beak and wattle are pink. Young males of the breed usually weigh about 25 pounds (11.3 kg) and young females about 16 pounds (7.25 kg) on average.

Chapter Three: What to Know Before You Buy

Now that you know a few of the basics about heritage turkeys, you may feel ready to make the big decision – are they the right pet for you? Knowing the basics may not be enough, however. You also have to know whether you need a license to keep turkeys, how many to buy and whether they can be kept with other animals. You would also be wise to familiarize yourself with the costs of purchasing and keeping heritage turkeys. In this chapter you will find all of this information and more so you can make a truly educated decision.

1.) Do You Need a License?

Before you go out and buy a heritage turkey or two, you need to make sure that it is legal to keep them in your area. Most countries have laws and regulations regarding the types of animal you can legally keep or breed, so you will need to check on the particular legislation in your area as it pertains to heritage turkeys. The last thing you want is to purchase your heritage turkeys and then have them taken away because you didn't follow legal regulations.

a.) Licensing in the U.S.

In the United States, licensing requirements for pets vary from one state to another. While some states have very strict requirements, others can be very lax. What you need to be careful about in regard to keeping turkeys is that the laws may be different for keeping wild turkeys than they are for domestic breeds like heritage turkeys. These requirements are set in place to prevent the spread of disease between wild and domestic birds.

Getting a license for keeping heritage turkeys is different than getting a permit for a traditional pet like a dog or cat because heritage turkeys are considered domestic fowl or livestock. Permit regulations are different for livestock than they are for pets and you may be subject to certain zoning requirements depending where you live. If you live in a rural area, the requirements may be less strict than if you live in a city – some cities prohibit the keeping or breeding of livestock while others simply limit the number you can keep on a certain amount of land.

In order to legally keep heritage turkeys you will need to check with your local office for regulations regarding the number of turkeys you can keep and how much space is required. Many areas have requirements for enclosure size, ventilation and sanitation. You will have to apply for a permit and renew that permit each year that you keep your turkeys – failure to do so could result in fines. Depending on the area in which you live, you may also have to follow certain regulations for tagging your turkeys.

b.) Licensing in the U.K.

In 2006, the Department for Environment, Food and Rural Affairs (DEFRA) issued the Animal Welfare Act. This act set forth legislation and regulations for the protection of animals, providing guidance for pet owners to ensure the proper treatment of pets. Under the Animal Welfare Act, pets must be provided with suitable and clean accommodation; appropriate food and drink; and adequate protection from harm including disease and fire.

In addition to outlining regulations for the welfare of pets, DEFRA has also issued regulations in regard to the farming of poultry including heritage turkeys. All poultry must be registered on the Great Britain Poultry Register if you stock 50 or more birds on your farm – even if the farm is only stocked during part of the year. If you keep fewer than 50 turkeys, you are not legally required to register them but it is recommended that you do so. If you keep other domestic fowl besides turkeys, the registration requirement of 50 birds refers to the total, not just one species.

In order to register your birds you will need to provide your contact information as well as a County Parish Holding Number. You will also need to describe the type of housing you provide your turkeys with as well as an explanation as to why you are keeping them. These questions are designed to assess the risk for disease transmission between flocks, particularly if your turkeys are exposed to wild birds.

2.) How Many Should You Buy?

As is true of most birds, turkeys are social animals that tend to thrive in flocks. While you may be able to raise a single turkey as a pet, they tend to do much better when kept with at least one other turkey. If you have the space, it would be wise for you to raise your turkeys in a group (or flock) – you just need to be careful about sexing the turkeys. Male and female turkeys can be kept together at a ratio of one male per six to eight females. If you try to keep two males together without enough females to go between them, they may end up fighting.

3.) Can Heritage Turkeys Be Kept with Other Pets?

When keeping heritage turkeys outdoors, you need to be particularly careful about keeping their food and water away from wild birds. Wild birds can carry disease and pests that may contaminate the enclosure and make your turkeys sick. Aside from wild birds, however, heritage turkeys can be kept with other domestic species including chickens and ducks.

There is a great deal of controversy regarding this subject, however, because it is possible for diseases to be transmitted from chickens to turkeys and vice versa. Many poultry keepers raise their chickens and turkeys together, however, with no problems. The key to keeping turkeys with other fowl is to ensure proper sanitation practices and to vaccinate your birds against diseases like blackhead, particularly if the risk is high in your region. Feeding your flocks food that has been medicated against blackhead may help to prevent the disease before it even becomes a problem for you.

4.) Ease and Cost of Care

In addition to knowing the basics about heritage turkeys as a breed, you should also learn about some of the practical aspects of caring for them. How much does it cost to buy a turkey and what other costs can you expect at the startup? Caring for a pet can be expensive and unless you are fully prepared and able to cover all of the costs required, you should not purchase the animal. In this section you will learn the basics about the initial and monthly costs for keeping heritage turkeys as pets.

a.) Initial Costs

The initial costs of heritage turkeys as pets include the purchase price of the bird, the cost to create and furnish the enclosure and any initial veterinary care your bird may require – this includes beak or feather trimming as well as vaccinations against disease. Below you will find a list and detailed explanations of each initial cost for keeping heritage turkeys as pets.

Purchase Price – When it comes to buying heritage turkeys, you have several options available. You can purchase an adult bird from a breeder if you simply plan to keep the bird as a pet. If you want to breed your turkeys, however, you would be better off purchasing eggs or newly hatched poults. When purchasing poults, the cost may vary depending on the breed and the number you purchase – many breeders offer a discount for certain quantities. Generally, you should expect to pay between $3 and $10 (£1.95 - £6.50) per poult or egg. For an adult turkey, you might pay between $25 and $50 (£16.25 - £32.50).

Brooder – If you plan to purchase your turkeys as poults, you will need to house them in a brooder until they are large enough for a traditional pen. A brooder can be made at home for as little as $10 (£6.50), or you can purchase a large commercial brooder for upwards of $1,000 (£650). For the sake of budgeting, plan to spend between $20 and $100 (£13 - £65) on a brooder.

Enclosure – Once your turkey poults are large enough to be moved to a pen, you will need to keep them securely housed. You have the option of keeping your turkeys inside our outside and each option has its benefits and drawbacks. Regardless where you keep your turkeys, you will need to invest in some high-quality fencing to keep your turkeys in and predators out. You can plan to pay between $50 and

$150 per roll of fencing plus an additional $100 or more for a charger if you plan to use electric fencing. You may also choose to house your turkeys in a barn or similar structure which could cost several thousand dollars to build if you do not already have one to use. For a large turkey pen, plan to spend $300 to $3,000 (£195 - £1950)

Furnishings – In addition to the enclosure itself, you also need to provide your turkeys with places to roost – these may be as simple as a bale of hay on which they can perch or a rod attached to the pen wall. In addition to roosting sites you will need to provide your turkeys with feeding and watering equipment. You can purchase an automated water fount for as little as $20 (£13) and may be able to use simple trays for feeding your turkeys, unless you keep them outdoors. Turkeys kept outdoors require special feeders that will not attract wild birds. Generally, you should budget between $50 and $200 (£32.50 - £130) to furnish your turkey pen.

Veterinary Care – As long as you purchase your turkeys from a reputable breeder, you shouldn't haven't to worry too much about initial veterinary care. You may, however, want to consider vaccinating your turkeys against certain diseases before you bring them home – particularly if they are at high risk in your area. The cost to vaccinate a turkey can be fairly low, especially if you purchase the vaccine at a farm supply store and administer it yourself. You can expect to pay about $5 to $10 per vaccine (£3.25 - £6.50).

For an overview of the initial costs of keeping heritage turkeys, consult the table below. The costs are divided into two columns – one column for a single turkey and second column for a trio of turkeys. All costs are estimated and may vary depending on your region.

Initial Costs for Heritage Turkeys		
Cost	**Single**	**Trio**
Purchase (Poult)	$3 to $10 (£1.95 - £6.50)	$9 to $30 (£5.85 - £19.50)
Purchase (Adult)	$25 to $50 (£16.25 - £32.50)	$75 and $150 (£48.75 - £97.50)
Brooder	$20 to $100 (£13 - £65)	$20 to $100 (£13 - £65)
Enclosure	$300 to $3,000 (£195 - £1950)	$300 to $3,000 (£195 - £1950)
Furnishings	$50 to $200 (£32.50 - £130)	$50 to $200 (£32.50 - £130)
Veterinary Cost	$5 to $10	$15 to $30

		(£3.25 - £6.50)	(£9.75 - £19.50)
		$403 to $3,370	$469 to $3,510
	Total	(£262 – £2191)	(£306 - £2282)

b.) Monthly Costs

Once you have purchased your heritage turkeys and set them up with their enclosure your job isn't finished – it is only just beginning. From this point on you must cover certain monthly costs for the upkeep and feeding of your turkeys. Some of the monthly costs you can expect include the cost of food, bedding, repairs and replacement of materials – you may even want to budget in the cost of emergency veterinary care. Below you will find a list and detailed explanations of each monthly cost for keeping heritage turkeys as pets.

Food – Feeding costs for heritage turkey vary greatly depending on where you house them. If you house your turkeys outdoors, your feeding costs may be lower because your turkeys will naturally forage for food like insects. You will still have to provide your turkeys with a high-quality feed, however.

During the first five weeks of their lives, turkey poults will need a special "starter formula" – after that point, they can move on to a high-protein rearing/growing formula. The average cost for a 50-pound bag of turkey feed is about $40 (£26) and you can expect to go through 5 to 8 bags of feed per turkey per year, averaging to a cost of about $250 (£162.50) per turkey per year. For the sake of calculating monthly costs, this rounds down to about $21 (£14) per month.

Bedding – Whether or not you need bedding for your turkey pen depends on whether you are keeping them indoors or outdoors. Even if you keep your turkeys outside, however, you will need to line nesting boxes with bedding to make them comfortable for your hens. For the most part, clean straw or wood shavings make the best bedding for turkeys and you should be able to buy this bedding in bulk at your local farm supply store for a total cost around $30 (£19.50) per month or less.

Repairs/Replacements – You always need to be prepared to make repairs to your turkey pen or to replace certain items like feeders or watering units. Generally, you won't have to do this on a monthly basis but it is a good idea to keep it in mind when planning your budget. For the sake of preparation, include about $10 (£6.50) per month in repairs and replacements for your turkey pen.

Emergency Vet – The cost of taking your turkey to the vet for emergency care can be quite high – much higher than the cost of purchasing your turkey in the first place. You also have to consider the cost of medications and the fact that turkeys often do not respond well to treatment. This being the case, many poultry farmers choose to cull their sick turkeys to prevent them from spreading disease to others in the flock. If you are simply in need of a veterinary checkup, however, or just want a second opinion on something that is going on with your turkeys, you should expect to pay about $65 (£42.25) per visit. In order to calculate a monthly cost, one visit divided by 12 months would only average to about $5 (£3.25) per month.

For an overview of the monthly costs of keeping heritage turkeys, consult the table below. The costs are divided into two columns – one column for a single turkey and second column for a trio of turkeys. All costs are estimated and may vary depending on your region.

Monthly Costs for Heritage Turkeys		
Cost	Single	Trio
Food	$21 (£14)	$63 (£41)
Bedding	$30 (£19.50)	$30 (£19.50)
Repairs	$10 (£6.50)	$10 (£6.50)
Emergency Vet	$5 (£3.25)	$15 (£9.75)
Total	$66 (£43)	$91 (£59)

5.) *Pros and Cons of Heritage Turkeys*

The last thing you need to do before you truly decide whether heritage turkeys are the right pet for you is to familiarize yourself with the pros and cons of keeping them. Every pet has its associated advantages and disadvantages but you need to be fully prepared before you take the big step in buying one. In this section you will find a detailed list of the pros and cons associated with heritage turkeys in particular so you can make a truly informed decision for yourself.

Pros of Heritage Turkeys

- Ten different breeds to choose from
- Very colorful and attractive animals – wide range in appearance
- Generally hardy, can have a long and productive life outdoors
- Adaptable to indoor environments with proper space and enrichment
- Can be raised and bred in flocks, either indoors or outdoors

- Eggs can be sold or consumed if you don't plan to raise the chicks
- With proper enrichment, can be very entertaining pets
- Much more active and intelligent than commercially bred turkeys
- Able to breed naturally – no need for artificial insemination

Cons of Heritage Turkeys

- Require significant space, particularly for flocks
- If kept outdoors, require secure fencing to protect against predators
- Birds kept indoors require secure pens with soft bedding and enrichment opportunities
- If kept outdoors, may be at increased risk for disease and pest infestations
- Require routine vaccination and veterinary care to prevent the spread of disease
- Beaks and feathers must be trimmed from an early age (10 days old)

Chapter Four: Purchasing Heritage Turkeys

By now you should have a pretty good idea what to expect when keeping heritage turkeys as a pet. You may also be ready to move on to thinking about actually buying one. In this chapter you will find the information you need to buy heritage turkeys as well as some tips for picking out turkeys that are healthy.

1.) Where to Buy Heritage Turkeys

If you have decided that heritage turkeys are the right choice of pet for you, you should start to think about where you are going to get one. Your best bet is to purchase from an experienced breeder because you are more likely to get a turkey or poult that has been bred from high quality stock. When it comes to buying heritage turkeys, you have the option to purchase adult birds or newly hatched poults. You can also buy the eggs and hatch them yourself.

a.) Buying in the U.S.

In the United States there are many heritage turkey breeders to choose from. Simply perform an online search or ask your local farm veterinarian for recommendations. Some sites you might try include:

Pauley's Rowdy Acres
<http://pauleysrowdyacres.com/sales.html>

Porter's Rare Heritage Turkeys
<http://www.porterturkeys.com/poultorderinginfo.htm>

Arriola Sunshine Farm.

<http://www.arriolasunshinefarm.com/heritage-turkey.html>

b.) Buying in the U.K.

Buying a heritage turkey in the United Kingdom is very similar to buying in the U.S. – you just have to find a reputable breeder. If you know someone who keeps heritage turkeys, ask them for a referral or consult your local farm vet for a recommendation. You can also perform an online search or try one of these breeders:

Rutland Organic Turkeys

<http://www.rutlandorganics.co.uk/rutland-heritage-turkeys.html>

HeritageTurkeys.co.uk

<http://www.heritageturkeys.co.uk/shop.aspx>

Sanderson's Poultry

<http://david.redmoosemedia.co.uk/breeds/heritage/black-winged-bronze>

2.) *How to Select a Healthy Heritage Turkey*

If you are ready to buy a heritage turkey, you want to be sure that the bird you bring home is in good health. Unfortunately, if you buy eggs or poults you may not be able to tell right away. If you choose to buy an adult, bird, however, you can observe and examine the turkey for signs of health. Before you buy, use the following tips to select a reputable breeder:

- Speak to the breeder directly over the phone
- Ask plenty of questions about the breeder's experience and breeding practices

- Ask the breeder if he has records of his breeding stock – they must all be naturally bred to be heritage turkeys
- See what breeds the breeder has available and make sure he is knowledgeable about the differences
- Ask to take a tour of the breeding facilities – you should make sure they are clean and well maintained
- Spend some time with the birds, observing them for signs of healthy behavior
- Ask questions about health guarantees and ask the breeder for a referral to other customers

Once you determine that the breeder is reputable and seems to know what he is doing, you can take the next step in purchasing your bird. If you are buying an adult bird, you may be able to pick out the bird you want and have the breeder put it on hold for you. If you are purchasing poults or eggs, you might be able to select the breeding pair. In some cases, however, you may only be able to pick the breed or color combination you are interested in.

3.) Heritage Turkeys as Food

As it has already been mentioned, Heritage Turkeys are not just popular as pets – they are also a popular food source. Turkey has long been a holiday feast item, though the birds can really be used any time of year. In this section you will learn the basics about Heritage Turkeys as food, including a few tasty recipes.

a.) Benefits of Heritage Turkeys

In recent years there has been a movement toward natural and organic foods. While commercially produced turkeys are artificially bred and loaded with hormones, Heritage Turkeys are all natural. This makes them a popular choice among people who are environmentally or morally conscious when it comes to their food choices. Fortunately, Heritage Turkeys are becoming more readily available as pets and as food so it is fairly easy to find them.

Some of the benefits of Heritage Turkeys include:

- Naturally bred, no artificial insemination

- Raised on a natural diet free from pesticides and hormones
- Naturally healthier, not loaded with antibiotics
- More dark meat than light meat
- Better flavor and lower risk for salmonella
- Typically sold fresh, not frozen or preserved

b.) Tips for Buying Heritage Turkey

The main thing you need to keep in mind when purchasing a Heritage Turkey over a commercially raised turkey is that there is going to be a difference in price. Heritage Turkeys can cost upwards of $6 (£3.90) per pound while commercially raised birds average around $1.50 (£1) per pound. Don't let the price throw you – that is your first tip for buying Heritage Turkey. Think about all of the benefits listed above that Heritage Turkeys have over commercially raised birds and you may find that the higher price is quite justified.

If you have decided to purchase a Heritage Turkey, you may be wondering where to find one. Try your local health food store or see if there is an organic food co-op in your area. You might even check the newspaper for local farms advertising Heritage Turkeys. Keep in mind that if you do buy a Heritage Turkey, it is likely to be fresh – not frozen like the commercially raised birds – so plan your purchase accordingly in order to cook it so it is fresh.

c.) Heritage Turkey Recipes

Below you will find three unique and delicious recipes specially designed for Heritage Turkeys.

Roasted Turkey with Maple Rosemary Butter

Ingredients:
1 (15 lbs.) fresh Heritage Turkey, room temperature
Salt and pepper to taste
2 cups water
2 cups white wine
1 bay leaf
½ lbs. salted sweet cream butter, softened
½ cup pure maple syrup
1 tablespoon fresh rosemary, minced

Directions:

1. Remove the giblets from the turkey and rinse the bird inside and out with cool water.
2. Pat the bird dry with paper towel then season liberally with salt and pepper – inside and out.
3. Combine the butter, maple syrup and rosemary in a bowl and whip until well combined.
4. Rub the rosemary butter into the meat of the bird, under the skin, and inside the cavity.
5. Place the bird in a deep roasting pan.
6. Whisk together the water, white wine and bay leaf in a small saucepan and bring to a simmer.
7. Add the giblets and simmer for 15 minutes then discard the bay leaf.
8. Pour the liquid into the pan around the turkey and top the turkey with a piece of greased foil.
9. Preheat the oven to 425°F.
10. Roast the turkey until it reaches an internal temperature of 140°F-150°F.
11. Remove the turkey to a cutting board and let rest for 10 to 15 minutes before carving.

Roasted Turkey with Cider Gravy

Cider Gravy Ingredients:

2 ½ cups diced celery

2 cups chopped yellow onion

6 sprigs fresh thyme

½ cup apple cider

2 tablespoons apple cider vinegar

¼ teaspoon whole black peppercorns

8 cups chicken broth

Turkey Ingredients:

1 (18 lbs.) fresh Heritage Turkey

Salt and pepper to taste

1 stick unsalted butter, softened

2 cups diced celery

2 cups coarsely chopped onion

2 cups chopped carrots

½ cup olive oil

3 bay leaves

2 sprigs fresh sage

½ cup all-purpose flour

To Prepare the Gravy Base:

1. Preheat the oven to 425°F.
2. Stir together the celery, onions, thyme and peppercorns for the gravy base in an oven-proof pot.
3. Roast, uncovered, for 10 minutes.

4. Stir in the apple cider and cider vinegar then reduce temperature to 375°F.
5. Whisk in the chicken stock and roast for 1 ½ hours, uncovered.
6. Strain the mixture and reserve the liquid, about 5 cups.

To Prepare the Turkey:

1. Remove the giblets from the turkey and rinse the bird inside and out with cool water.
2. Pat the bird dry with paper towel then season liberally with salt and pepper – inside and out.
3. Rub the butter into the turkey meat beneath the skin then place the turkey in a deep roasting pan.
4. Set the oven rack in the lowest position and preheat to 350°F.
5. Combine the vegetables and herbs in a bowl with the oil and toss well – pour the vegetables into the roasting pan around the turkey.
6. Roast the turkey until the internal temperature at the thickest portion is about 165°F, basting every 30 minutes.
7. Spoon the vegetables and the drippings from the turkey into a strainer over a large bowl.
8. Skim the fat from the drippings, reserving about 1 cup of the liquid and ¼ cup of the fat.

9. Heat the fat in a large saucepan over medium heat then whisk in the flour.

10. Gradually whisk in the cider gravy base and the 1 cup pan drippings.

11. Simmer the mixture, whisking often, until smooth and heated through.

12. Season with salt and pepper to taste and serve with the turkey.

Traditional Herb-Roasted Turkey

Ingredients:

1 (15 to 18 lbs.) fresh Heritage Turkey, room temperature

¼ cup unsalted butter, softened

Salt and pepper to taste

12 sprigs fresh thyme

6 sprigs fresh sage

2 bay leaves

2 medium apples, sliced

1 medium sweet onion, sliced

Directions:

1. Remove the giblets from the turkey and rinse the bird inside and out with cool water.

2. Pat the bird dry with paper towel then season liberally with salt and pepper – inside and out.
3. Rub the butter into the meat of the bird under the skin.
4. Preheat the oven to 475°F and place the oven rack in the lowest position.
5. Fill the cavity with the herbs, onion and apple then tie the legs together, tucking them close to the body.
6. Place the turkey in a deep roasting pan and add the water to the pan.
7. Roast for 20 minutes then reduce the oven temperature to 400°F and baste the turkey with its juices.
8. Continue to roast the turkey for about 2 to 2 ½ hours longer until the internal temperature reaches about 160°F at the thickest portion (the breast).
9. Remove the turkey to a cutting board and let rest for 20 minutes before carving.

Chapter Five: Caring for Heritage Turkeys

Once you bring your heritage turkey home, the hard work begins – you are now solely responsible for their care and wellbeing. The health of your heritage turkeys will be determined by a number of factors, primarily their habitat and diet. In this chapter you will learn how to create the ideal habitat for your heritage turkeys and how to craft a healthy diet for them. After reading this chapter you will be ready to give your turkeys the best care possible.

1.) Habitat Requirements

Heritage turkeys are fairly easy to keep because their habitat requirements are not complicated. For the most part, all you have to do is provide your turkeys with plenty of open space and protection from wild animals. In this section you will learn all of the basics about providing a clean and healthy habitat for your turkeys to ensure that they remain in good health.

a.) Space Requirements

Heritage turkeys are not terribly large birds, but they are very active and do require a significant amount of space. The more space you provide for your turkeys, the happier and healthier they will be. According to the American Livestock Breeders Conservancy, a 1-acre plot of land is sufficient to house 100 heritage turkeys – this averages to about 435 square feet per turkey (133 square km). A fenced-in pasture is ideal for raising turkeys because it provides plenty of open space as well as foraging opportunities.

If you plan to keep your turkeys indoors, you will need to build them a barn or some kind of shelter. Space recommendations for turkeys kept indoors varies – you may be able to get away with something about 20-by-40 feet but a larger area measuring about 1/8 acre or 75-by-75 feet (22.8x22.8 m) is better. If you have a large wooden barn, that would be ideal for an indoor turkey pen. Alternatively, you can use a large garage or shed.

b.) Building Materials

If you already have a barn, shed or garage in place you may not have to worry about actually constructing much for your turkeys. For those who are building their turkey enclosure, however, certain materials are recommended. For flooring, wood covered with rubber mats or some kind of bedding is best. Though plain wooden flooring is easy for cleaning, your turkeys could slip on the slick material. Be sure to provide plenty of clean straw or wood shavings for bedding to keep your turkeys' feet dry.

Even if you keep your turkeys outdoors, you will need to provide them with some kind of shelter at night. The purpose of this shelter is not just to keep the turkeys protected from the weather, but also to keep them out of harm's way from predators. You will need to make sure the shelter is secure, able to keep out predators as well as rats – it should also keep out wild birds because they can transmit diseases to your turkeys. Make sure the floor is lined with bedding to keep your birds comfortable overnight.

For outdoor enclosures, you will need to secure the perimeter with some kind of fencing. You may choose whether to use traditional fencing or electric fencing – many poultry farmers use a combination of both. To use a combination, make a perimeter out of electric fencing then divide the pasture into smaller portions using regular fencing. This will protect your birds from the electricity and will also ensure that you can rotate them throughout the various sections of your pasture to keep them fresh.

c.) Selecting the Right Fencing

Not only does the fencing in your turkey enclosure need to keep your birds in, but it also needs to keep predators out. For larger breeds of heritage turkey and those whose wings have been clipped, fencing may only need to be about 5 feet (1.5m) high. To be safe, however, a fence height of 6 feet (1.8m) is recommended. If you are keeping multiple flocks in adjacent pens (particularly for the purpose of breeding), you will need to cover the bottom half of the adjoining fence so the males can't fight with each other through the fence.

In addition to height, you also need to think about the right material for your fencing. Chicken wire is not recommended because it is too flimsy – your turkeys could break free or predators could get into the pen. The best type of fencing for turkeys is a woven "no climb" fence that can be stretched tight around a perimeter of vertical wooden poles. You also may want to think about digging a trench and burying a portion of the fence to keep out digging predators like foxes.

d.) Maintenance Tips

In addition to providing your heritage turkeys with the right habitat, you also have to keep it clean. This is particularly important for turkeys being kept indoors because waste and debris can accumulate quickly. If you do not clean your turkey's pen often enough it could cause your turkeys to become stressed and they will be at a greater risk for contracting disease.

Most poultry farmers recommended cleaning the entire turkey pen and shelter once a week. You will need to remove all bedding and scrub the walls and floors thoroughly with a mild disinfectant. It is important that you let everything dry before you replenish the bedding and put the turkeys back in the pen. In addition to cleaning the pen itself you will also need to clean and disinfect feeders, watering equipment and other accessories.

e.) Summary of Facts

Birds per Acre: about 100

Space per Bird: 435 square feet (133 square km)

Indoor Pen Size: ideally 1/8 acre or 75-by-75 feet (22.8x22.8 m)

Flooring: wood covered with rubber mats or bedding

Bedding: clean straw or wood shavings

Shelter: necessary for indoor and outdoor turkeys

Shelter Types: shed, barn, garage

Preferred Fencing: woven "no climb" fencing; chicken wire not recommended

Maintenance: full cleaning of pen and shelter weekly; clean and disinfect feeders, water equipment and accessories

2.) Feeding Heritage Turkeys

a.) Nutritional Needs

In order to create a diet for your heritage turkeys, you need to have a basic understanding of their nutritional needs. Like all living things, turkeys need access to plenty of clean water. The ideal way to provide water for turkeys is through an automatic water fountain. These units help to prevent spillage and ensure that the water is always fresh. Even with an automatic unit, however, you will need to refresh the water daily and keep the unit clean.

The basis of a heritage turkey's diet should come from high-quality pellet feed. It is important to note that turkeys have a higher need for protein than other poultry like chickens, so you need to buy feed that is formulated specifically for turkeys. Be careful when buying turkey feed because the cheaper the product, the lower the quality. Many food manufacturers use low-quality ingredients as fillers to increase the bulk of their product without actually adding any nutritional value. You may want to consider organic turkey feed because this will provide your turkeys with the best nourishment possible.

When your turkeys are newly hatched, they require a starter diet that consists of between 24% and 28% protein. If possible, offer your poults feed with 28% protein for the first four weeks then scale back to 24% for the next four. After eight weeks of age, the poults can be given feed with a 20% protein ratio. In addition to protein, newly hatched poults also require specific amino acids like lysine and methionine, particularly during the first six weeks of life.

Once your turkeys reach sexual maturity around 28 weeks, they can be switched to a feed with about 17% protein. At this point it is important to find a feed that provides a variety of vitamins and minerals – a balance of calcium and phosphorus is also essential for proper bone health. For mature birds, it is best to find a feed that has a higher fiber content than would a starter formula because you do not want the birds to put on too much extra fat. High protein levels in breeding birds may also contribute to reduced hatchability rates.

b.) How Much to Feed

For the most part, you do not have to worry about giving your turkeys a specific amount of food – they will feed freely and forage for insects as well. The ideal way to feed turkeys is to buy a trough or hopper-style feeder. These units are available in multiple sizes and they are designed to protect the feed from wind and rain – they also keep the turkeys from walking or sleeping in the feed. If you are housing your turkeys outside, it is especially important that you buy a feeder that will keep out wild birds.

The feeders themselves need to be set up off the ground at a height level with the bird's back. When your turkeys are still young you will need to have the feeders closer to the ground and increase the height as they grow. You also need to think about how much space your feeders provide per bird, since they will often feed side by side. For young poults up to six weeks old you should provide about 2 to 3 linear inches (5 to 7 cm) of space per poult. For adult birds, you will need at least 6 inches (15 cm) of linear space or more.

The amount of feed your turkeys consume will vary by age and size. A 1-2 week-old poult may consume about ¼ lbs. (.11 kg) of feed per week while a 3-4 week-old poult may eat more than three times that much. As the poults mature, they continue to eat more – up to 4 pounds of feed per week by the time they reach 22 weeks of age. Once the turkeys reach maturity around 28 weeks of age they may reach an average consumption around 4 ½ lbs. (2 kg) of feed per week. Again, your turkeys will eat as they are hungry so you do not need to ration the food per bird – just make sure there is plenty of fresh feed available at all times.

c.) Types of Food

When it comes to commercial turkey feed, there are generally three different formulas for pellets: starter feed, growing feed and finishing feed. These formulas may have slightly different names but they are specifically designed for turkeys at certain stages of life. Starter feed, also called "crumbs," is high in protein and provides poults with the nutrients they need to grow. Growing feed helps to support older birds as they mature with a slightly lower protein content. Once birds reach sexual maturity they need less protein and more fiber to maintain their weight.

d.) Summary of Facts

Water: automatic water fountain
Feeder: trough or hopper-style, raised off the ground
Feeding Space (poults): 2 to 3 inches (5 to 7 cm) per bird
Feeding Space (adults): 6 linear inches (15 cm) per bird
Feed Formulas: starter feed, growing feed, finishing feed
Protein Content (poults): 28% first 4 weeks, 24% next 4
Protein Content (adults): 20% until sexual maturity (28 weeks), then 17% protein
Additional Nutrients: calcium, phosphorus, B vitamins, trace minerals

3.) Farming Heritage Turkeys

In addition to being kept as pets, Heritage Turkeys can also be farmed for meat, eggs and feathers. Heritage birds are definitely rising in popularity, but it is important to keep in mind that the cost of raising these birds is different from the cost of commercial breeds. Commercial breeds are selectively bred to produce as much breast meat as possible (thus increasing their value at sale) and they are also pumped full of hormones to make them grow quickly. Heritage Turkeys take about 28 weeks to mature while commercial breeds mature around 12 weeks.

These are just a few of the things you need to consider when farming Heritage Turkeys. Some other things to think about include:

- Costs for housing your turkeys – they should be kept outside and thus need protection from predators
- High-quality feed – preferably organic (supplemented by foraging for insects)
- Purchasing Heritage Turkeys to start farming is more expensive than commercial breeds
- Labor costs and time are about the same as for commercially raised birds

- Gross income per bird is higher at sale
- Demand for smaller birds may be increasing – could be beneficial for Heritage Turkey sales

Heritage Turkeys can be farmed at home for a number of different reasons. For many people, it is as much about preserving heritage breeds as it is about making money off of them. Some people simply raise the birds for the use of their family and friends. Some of the most popular Heritage Turkey breeds for farming include Standard Bronze and Narragansett. Bourbon Red turkeys are great for foraging and they are a popular medium-sized bird. For smaller turkeys, the Royal Palm is particularly popular.

What you choose to do with your Heritage Turkeys is up to you – you can gather and sell the eggs or you can hatch and sell the chicks. You can also raise the chicks to maturity and sell the birds for meat. Regardless how you choose to use your Heritage Turkeys, it is essential that you follow healthy and humane farming practices – that is what sets Heritage Turkey farmers apart from factory farmers.

Chapter Six: Breeding Heritage Turkeys

Over the past few centuries, the food industry has come to dominate the breeding of turkeys but individuals and small farms around the world continue to breed heritage turkeys. Breeding heritage turkeys isn't just about producing food or cultivating more pets, it is about preserving the unique and beautiful creatures that they are. In this chapter you will learn everything you need to know about breeding heritage turkeys including choosing breeding stock, preparing your birds for breeding and raising the babies.

1.) Basic Breeding Info

Before you attempt to breed your heritage turkeys, you need to be sure that your breeding stock is of the highest quality. This will not only ensure that the babies are healthy and sound, but it will also ensure that the coloration and patterns of the babies are consistent with the breed standard. Plumage color is only one of the many traits passed on from adults to their young, so there are many factors to consider in choosing your breeding stock.

Some factors to consider in choosing breeding stock may include:

- Select specimens that meet the criteria for the particular breed (ex: Bourbon Red)
- Choose birds that are vigorous and in good health – unhealthy birds may not be able to handle the rigors of breeding
- Only choose birds that have come from a line of naturally mated birds – no artificial insemination
- Choose a hen that has a good record for laying quality eggs with a good hatching rate
- Select a male of good size that has produced healthy, attractive young
- Choose a pair that will produce the colors and patterns you are looking for (this may require some research on your part)

In addition to selecting high quality breeding stock, you also need to think about the specifics of breeding. While many animals mate in a 1:1 ratio (one male to one female), heritage turkeys tend to breed better in groups. The ideal ratio seems to be about one male per six or eight females. It is also possible to breed your turkeys in flocks, using multiple males for a larger number of females. When breeding your turkeys in groups like this it is essential that you provide plenty of open space to minimize fighting.

If you are breeding your heritage turkeys purely for your own enjoyment, either of the options above will work. If you plan to sell your turkeys, however, you may want to go with the option of only one male per group of females because this will make record-keeping much easier. When breeding heritage turkeys in large flocks, you may not be able to keep track of which male fertilizes which female. People who want to buy turkeys from you, particularly if they intend to breed them themselves, will be interested in the lineage of the birds they buy.

2.) The Breeding Process

Female heritage turkeys (hens) are capable of laying eggs starting around the age of 28 weeks. The number of eggs produced tends to be highest in the first year of production, decreasing slightly from each year thereafter. This is also true of males in the sense that they are most fertile during their first year – this is why turkey breeders tend to prefer young males in producing poults that are intended for sale. Older males may still be capable of breeding, but they will produce a smaller number of fertile eggs.

It is not recommended that you keep male and female heritage turkeys together in the same pen except during breeding periods. Several months before the laying season begins, however, you should introduce the two sexes – be sure to provide plenty of room for this because the male likes to herd his females around. It is also essential that you feed your birds a high-quality breeders' pellet at this time to maximize the health of your breeding stock.

When breeding your heritage turkeys, you do not need to keep them indoors – an outdoor pen is just fine as long as it is fenced to protect the birds from predators. If you keep your turkeys outside, make sure their food is in an enclosed unit to prevent wild birds from eating it. You should also make sure that your watering containers are raised off the ground to prevent contamination. Your female turkeys can remain in the outdoor pen throughout the breeding season, but you will need to rotate out the male turkey once every week to give him a break in a pen on his own.

As an alternative to outdoor breeding, you can also breed your heritage turkeys indoors in pens. The pens themselves need to be at least 4 feet (1.2 m) high or higher, particularly if the birds haven't had their wings clipped. You can have multiple pens next to each other but at least the bottom half of the connecting pen walls need to be solid to prevent males from adjacent pens fighting. Even if you only have one group to breed, it is a good idea to have two pens so you can alternate between the two for easy cleaning.

Inside each breeding pen you will need to provide straw bales or perches – these perches should be no more than 18 inches (45 cm) off the ground. The ground itself should be lined with clean straw or wood shavings to absorb moisture and keep your turkeys' feet dry. You should also provide nest boxes for your female turkeys – in outdoor pens, place the nest boxes in the shadiest side of the pen.

Each nest box should measure about 18x18x24 inches (45x45x60cm) and you should provide one for each female. In addition to individual nest boxes you may also choose to provide a communal nest box – this may make it easier to collect the eggs. You can easily build your own nest boxes using plywood – just be sure the wood hasn't been treated with any chemicals that might be toxic to your turkeys.

Note: No matter where you have your breeding pen (indoors or outdoors), be sure to keep an eye on the hens because a male turkey can cause damage to a hen's back with his claws. Clip the claws before breeding and keep the spurs filed down.

3.) Raising the Babies

Heritage turkeys breed continuously throughout the laying season and each mating can produce between 10 and 12 fertile eggs. The number of eggs laid in a season depends on the size of the turkey – larger breeds may lay only 50 eggs in a season while smaller breeds might produce closer to 100. The laying season itself lasts between 16 and 20 weeks, beginning as early as March and tapering off by the end of June into August.

If you are breeding your turkeys for the eggs alone, you should plan to collect the eggs twice a day. If you intend to raise the chicks, however, you can leave the eggs in the nest box for the female to incubate. You can also remove the eggs and incubate them artificially – this leaves your hen free to produce another clutch. Before incubating the eggs you can let them rest in a cool pantry for up to one week but the rate of hatchability will decrease the longer you wait after laying.

a.) Incubating the Eggs

Before you place the eggs in the incubator, dip them in an egg sanitizer then allow them to come to room temperature. If you are using a commercial incubator (rather than homemade), you will be able to set the temperature and humidity for the eggs. The ideal temperature for incubating heritage turkey eggs is 99.5°F (37.5°C) with humidity around 55%. Let the eggs incubate for about one week then remove them one at a time to check for fertility.

One of the most popular methods of checking eggs for fertility is called candling. To use this method, simply remove one egg from the incubator and hold it up to a bright light. Eggs that are infertile will be clear – you won't see anything inside the egg. If the egg is fertile, however, you will see that the embryo inside the egg has begun to develop. Discard any eggs that are infertile.

After about 25 days in the incubator, you can reduce the temperature to 98.6°F (37°C). You should also increase the humidity level to about 75%. By day 28, the eggs should be ready to hatch. Do not rush the hatching process – it is important that you let the chicks break themselves out of the eggs. If you try to help a chick, you could end up opening the egg too soon and the chick could die. After the chicks have hatched you will need to let them dry completely then provide them with warmth, water and food.

b.) Raising the Chicks

The process of raising newly hatched chicks is called brooding. Unfortunately, turkey poults are notoriously tricky to get started on food and water after hatching but, with the right information, you can do it. Provide small amounts of heaped food spaced evenly around the brooding space – you can also use a small round feeder with a 55-pound (22 kg) capacity for every 25 chicks.

While food is important for the newly hatched chicks, water is even more essential. You will need to introduce the chicks to water by hand, carefully dipping their beaks in the water. You should only need one automatic water fountain per 50 poults. In addition to the water fountain, you may want to install small spotlights over the brooding area to attract the poults to the food at water. To further encourage your poults to eat, place the food in silver trays and, to encourage them to drink, place colored marbles in the water.

Turkey pouts can safely be raised in groups of up to 250. You will need to start trimming the poults' beaks around day 10 after hatching to prevent them from pecking each other – this is particularly important when keeping them in large groups. Continue to feed the poults and keep them well supplied with fresh water. By week 7, they can be moved outside and kept in smaller groups in an enclosure measuring at least 500 square feet per 10 birds.

Summary of Facts

Sexual Maturity: 24 to 28 weeks

Laying Season: March through August

Eggs per Year: 70 to 100

Chicks per Female: 43 to 63

Male to Female Ratio: 1:6, ideally (can also breed in flocks)

Egg Weight: average 85g

Incubation Period: 28 days

Indoor Breeding Pen: walls at least 4 feet (1.2 m) high

Adjacent Pens: bottom half solid fencing to prevent males from fighting

Bedding: straw or wood shavings

Accessories: straw bales or perches, nest boxes, feeder and watering equipment

Nest Box Dimension: 18x18x24 inches (45x45x60cm)

Incubation Temperature: 99.5°F (37.5°C)

Incubation Humidity: 55%

Fertility Check Method: candling after one week of incubation

Chapter Seven: Keeping Heritage Turkeys Healthy

As you already know, having healthy heritage turkeys starts with purchasing the turkey (or the eggs) from a reputable source. If your turkeys are healthy to begin with, you will mainly have to worry about disease prevention, not treatment. It would still be wise, however, to familiarize yourself with some of the most common diseases affecting these birds so you know how to handle them if they occur. In this chapter you will learn the basics about diseases affecting turkeys and how to handle them.

1.) *Common Health Problems*

Heritage turkeys are fairly hardy and tend to do well in a variety of environments. Providing them with a healthy diet and proper care, however, is essential for their well-being. If you care for your turkeys properly, you shouldn't have to worry about too many diseases affecting your flock. Just to be safe, however, it is a good idea to read up on common diseases affecting turkeys so you know how to identify the symptoms and what kind of treatment options you may need to consider.

Some of the most common diseases affecting heritage turkeys include:

Aspergillosis	Feather Picking
Avian Influenza	Fowl Cholera
Blackhead	Lice/Mites
Bumblefoot	Newcastle Disease
Coccidiosis	Roundworms
Dehydration	Turkey Pox

Aspergillosis

Also known as brooder pneumonia, this disease is a type of fungal infection caused by the fungus *Aspergillus fumigatus*. This disease most commonly affects young turkeys (poults) between one and eight weeks old. The fungus can be transmitted through spores from infected litter or feed and it is most common in crowded environments like brood houses.

The most common indications of this disease include heavy breathing and grey lesions in the throat, lungs and mouth. It is also possible for the lesions to occur in the eyes or brain. Unfortunately, there is no cure for this condition that is practical for use. The fungal spores are incredibly difficult to eradicate but increasing the humidity in the environment and removing the source of the infection may help. It is best to avoid using bark litters because they tend to retain moisture which can contribute to fungal infections.

Avian Influenza

Also known as AI, avian influenza is caused by a virus that has over 250 known strains. All birds are susceptible to avian influenza and the disease itself is found throughout the world. Only under certain circumstances, however, is the disease transmittable to humans. In many cases, this disease results from poor sanitation or close contact with wild birds that have been infected.

The early symptoms of this disease may include listlessness, respiratory distress and diarrhea – some birds may never even show any symptoms. In serious cases, symptoms may include dehydration, facial swelling, lesions and small hemorrhages. There is a vaccine available for this disease available for use during times of pandemic. There is no known treatment for this disease but the use of antibiotics may help to reduce losses from the infection.

Blackhead

Also called histomoniasis, this disease is caused by a protozoan called *Histomonas meleagridis*. In the early stages of the disease, turkeys may exhibit decreased appetite, drowsiness, increased thirst and dry-ruffled feathers. Mortality from this disease is particularly high among poults less than 12 weeks of age. Transmission occurs through direct contact with the protozoan eggs or indirectly through infected soil.

To deal with the disease, separate young birds from older birds and keep the enclosures as clean as possible. The most common treatment method is to feed medicated feed to the infected birds. As is true with many diseases affecting turkeys, treatment can be difficult and ineffective so prevention through good sanitation practices is the best option. In some cases, offering food treated with medication for Blackhead can also help to prevent the disease.

Bumblefoot

Bumblefoot, as the name suggests, is an infection affecting the foot. In most cases, the disease manifests as the hard swelling of the center of the foot pad – it may also affect the area between the toes. The skin on the foot pad and between the toes may begin to crack and, eventually, the infection could progress to the inside of the foot and even into the bone.

The most common cause of this condition is overcrowding and poor sanitation. Other factors which may contribute to the development of the disease include poor diet, hard flooring and roosts that are placed too high. If there are too many rocks or sharp objects in the enclosure, that could also contribute to the disease. Treatment for this condition involves covering flooring with soft bedding and medicating with antibiotics to treat the infection.

Coccidiosis

This is a disease caused by a protozoan parasite belonging to the genus *Elmeria*. Turkeys in particular are susceptible to 7 different strains of the parasite, though only 3 of them are known to be pathogenic. This disease is common in turkeys that are grown on a range or kept on litter. The parasites enter the body of the birds and produce cysts which are expelled through the feces. Contact with infected feces, particularly through ingestion of contaminated food or bedding, is the most common cause of infection.

The most common symptoms of this disease include weakness, ruffled feathers, drooping wings, listlessness and bloody diarrhea. There is a vaccine available against this disease, most commonly administered when birds are at risk for exposure to the parasite. Treatment for this disease may include an apple cider vinegar prophylactic treatment. Other medications may include sulphonamides, amprolium or toltrazuril.

Dehydration

Dehydration occurs when turkeys are not given proper access to fresh water. This could occur if you do not refill their water containers frequently enough or if you are using the wrong type of watering equipment. This is fairly common among young poults if they are introduced to a water source incorrectly or if there is insufficient watering space. Your turkeys could also stop drinking their water if it is contaminated.

Some indicators of dehydration include listlessness, white crystals around the vent, sunken appearance in the crop or empty crop. If your birds are dehydrated, you need to remedy the problems keeping them from drinking and then monitor them closely until they begin drinking well. If you recently added something to the water source preceding the onset of the problem, remove the additive. Be sure to provide your birds with plenty of fresh water at all times.

Feather Picking

Though not technically a disease, feather picking is a harmful condition which may affect turkeys. Signs of this condition include birds plucking their own feathers or the feathers of other birds – in some cases, this could escalate to attacking and injuring other birds in the flock. Some physical signs of this disease include bleeding or swelling, particularly near the vent, as a result of plucked feathers.

Stress is the most common cause of this condition, though bright light and insufficient diet can also contribute. If turkeys do not have enough space or if their environment lacks enrichment opportunities, they may become bored and stressed which can increase feather plucking behavior. The sight and smell of blood in other turkeys can also induce the behavior. To treat the disease, enlarge the enclosure and resolve the problems that are causing your birds to become stressed. Separate and treat injured birds until their wounds have healed.

Fowl Cholera

This disease is named "fowl" cholera because it affects all fowl including chickens, pheasants, ducks and turkeys. Caused by a bacteria called *Pasteurella multocida*, this infection tends to strike birds that are at least 6 weeks of age. Fowl cholera can result in sudden death but it can also cause fever, lethargy, increased water consumption and decreased appetite. Often, the disease causes sudden death in a few birds followed by the onset of fever and lethargy in other birds from the flock.

The bacteria known for causing this disease can live in soil or litter for months, though it can easily be killed using disinfectants or by exposure to direct sunlight. It is thought that wild birds are typically responsible for harboring and spreading the disease through infected feces and contaminated equipment. Sanitation is a key element in treatment as is the use of vaccines and control of rodents to prevent the disease from spreading. Medications for this disease may include sulphonamides, tetracyclines, penicillin or erythromycin. Unfortunately, the disease can recur after medication is stopped so long-term or periodic medication may be required.

Lice/Mites

There are about 40 different species of fowl lice and many different types of mites. These pests can reproduce quickly and multiple varieties can co-exist at one time on a single bird. Though lice and mites may not be pathogenic for adult birds, they can be very dangerous if poults become heavily infested. Evidence of lice or mite infestation may include skin blemishes, paleness, weakness, reduced food consumption and poor resistance to disease. In cases of extreme infestation, blood loss may result in anemia.

Proper sanitation is the key to preventing lice and mite infestations. Insecticides are available for the treatment of both the birds themselves and their housing, so it is important to treat the places where mites and lice are likely to hide. Once the infestation has cleared, it is essential that a thorough cleaning and disinfection be performed or the infestation will recur.

Newcastle Disease

Newcastle disease is incredibly contagious respiratory infection that can affect birds of all species. There are several different strains of the virus which is responsible for this disease, so symptoms and severity may vary from one case to another. Young birds are most susceptible to the disease and turkeys tend to be slightly more resistant to the disease than chickens.

The virus responsible for Newcastle disease typically affects the respiratory system, causing breathing problems – it may also affect the brain. If the disease comes on suddenly, it could result in decreased consumption of food and water.

Young birds have a high mortality rate from this disease. There are several ways to destroy the virus – exposure to heat or direct sunlight, fumigation or use of disinfectants. Vaccines are available for this disease.

Roundworms

Roundworms are a type of nematode parasite that tend to infect the intestinal tract. Some of the symptoms of this disease may include lack of vigor, weight loss, paleness, sagging wings, diarrhea and retarded growth rate in young birds. Young birds are most susceptible to this disease. The parasites responsible for this condition belong to the genus *Ascaridia* and there are several different forms which affect different types of birds.

This disease is contracted when turkeys ingest the eggs of the parasite as they eat contaminated food. The eggs then hatch in the intestine – it may take up to 5 or 10 weeks following ingestion for symptoms to present. Roundworm eggs can remain viable on contaminated surfaces and in soil for up to 1 year which makes controlling this disease difficult. Good sanitation practices are the key to prevention. Treatment typically involves medicated feed or treatment with medications like flubendazole.

Turkey Pox

Also referred to as Fowl Pox, turkey pox is caused by an infection transmitted by mosquitoes and other biting insects. It is also possible to transmit this disease through the ingestion of infected scabs or dust from an infected environment. Once a mosquito feeds on an infected bird, it can carry the disease for its entire life, spreading it as it feeds on other birds. This disease typically manifests with yellow lesions which can progress to thick scabs.

A vaccine is available for this disease, but it should only be used on farms and ranges where turkey pox is a recurrent problem. Unfortunately, there is no treatment for this disease, though some birds do recover on their own. Using antibiotic ointment on the scabs and adding antibiotics to the water can help to prevent secondary infections resulting from turkey pox.

2.) Preventing Illness

While providing your turkeys with a healthy diet and a clean environment is essential for keeping them healthy, there are other things you can do as well. Much as you would vaccinate a pet dog or cat, there are certain vaccines available for domestic fowl including turkeys. These vaccines can help to reduce your turkeys' risk for contracting a particularly disease.

It is important to note that these vaccines should not be administered without careful consideration – they are recommended only for turkeys that are at risk for the certain disease. To see whether your turkeys are at risk for certain diseases in your area, contact your local veterinarian. Some of the diseases for which vaccinations are available include turkey pox, avian encephalomyelitis, Newcastle disease and fowl cholera.

In addition to vaccinations and proper diet, it is important that your turkeys get plenty of exercise. Healthy turkeys should receive a varied diet of more than just the essentials and they should have plenty of space to move around. These things will help to prevent your turkeys from becoming stressed which will, in turn, keep their immune systems working to protect them from illness. It is also important that your turkeys have access to fresh, clean water at all times.

Chapter Eight: Heritage Turkeys Care Sheet

This book serves as a complete guide to the heritage turkey and, as such, you should find answers to all of your questions within its pages. There may come a time, however, when you need a quick answer to a simple question and you do not want to flip through the entire book. In cases like this, it is helpful to have a care sheet of relevant heritage turkey information. In this chapter you will find an overview of the most important facts about heritage turkeys as well as tips for creating a habitat, feeding your turkeys and breeding them.

1.) Basic Information

Scientific Name: Meleagris gollapavo
Breed Information: ten different breeds
Lifespan: 5 to 7 years average
Development Rate: market ready at 28 weeks
Qualifications: naturally mating, long productive outdoor lifespan, slow growth rate
Size (female): 12 to 16 lbs. (5.4 to 7.25 kg)
Size (male): 20 to 28 lbs. (9 to 12.7 kg)
Color: varies by species: white, brown, tan, slate, black, buff
Characteristics: hard pink or black beak, red or blueish head, pink or red wattle

2.) Habitat Set-Up Information

Birds per Acre: about 100
Space per Bird: 435 square feet (133 square km)
Indoor Pen Size: ideally 1/8 acre or 75-by-75 feet
Flooring: wood covered with rubber mats or bedding
Bedding: clean straw or wood shavings
Shelter: necessary for indoor and outdoor turkeys
Shelter Types: shed, barn, garage

Preferred Fencing: woven "no climb" fencing; chicken wire not recommended

Maintenance: full cleaning of pen and shelter weekly; clean and disinfect feeders, water equipment and accessories

3.) Care and Feeding Tips

Water: automatic water fountain

Feeder: trough or hopper-style, raised off the ground

Feeding Space (poults): 2 to 3 inches (5 to 7 cm) per bird

Feeding Space (adults): 6 linear inches (15 cm) per bird

Feed Formulas: starter feed, growing feed, finishing feed

Protein Content (poults): 28% first 4 weeks, 24% next 4

Protein Content (adults): 20% until sexual maturity (28 weeks), then 17% protein

Additional Nutrients: calcium, phosphorus, B vitamins, trace minerals

4.) Breeding Information

Sexual Maturity: 24 to 28 weeks

Laying Season: March through August

Eggs per Year: 70 to 100

Chicks per Female: 43 to 63

Male to Female Ratio: 1:6, ideally (can also breed in flocks)

Egg Weight: average 85g

Incubation Period: 28 days

Indoor Breeding Pen: walls at least 4 feet (1.2 m) high

Adjacent Pens: bottom half solid fencing to prevent males from fighting

Bedding: straw or wood shavings

Accessories: straw bales or perches, nest boxes, feeder and watering equipment

Nest Box Dimension: 18x18x24 inches (45x45x60cm)

Incubation Temperature: 99.5°F (37.5°C)

Incubation Humidity: 55%

Fertility Check Method: candling after one week of incubation

Chapter Nine: Frequently Asked Questions

After reading this book you may feel like an expert on the heritage turkey. If you ever have questions, you can simply flip back through the book to the appropriate section. If you are in need of a quick answer to a question, however, you might try looking through some of the most frequently asked questions made by new heritage turkey owners. You will find a list of these questions along with their answers in this chapter.

Q: *What qualifies a turkey as a heritage turkey?*

A: There are only 10 breeds of heritage turkey and they must meet three requirements: they must be naturally bred, live a productive outdoor life and they must have a slow growth rate.

Q: *How long do heritage turkeys live?*

A: Male heritage turkeys may only live 3 to 5 years but females can live up to 7 years or longer.

Q: *When can I start breeding my turkeys?*

A: Heritage turkeys are capable of laying eggs once they reach 28 weeks old. They are most fertile during their first year so, if you plan to breed your turkeys, you will get the best results while they are young.

Q: *What nutrients are most important in a diet for heritage turkeys?*

A: Particularly while your turkeys are young, protein is the nutrient they need most. As they grow you will lower the amount of protein in their diet in favor of more fiber but they should always have a feed with at least 17% protein.

Q: *Can I keep just one heritage turkey?*

A: You can keep a single heritage turkey but, like most birds, turkeys do best in groups (called flocks). The ideal situation would be to have a single male with 6 to 8 females but you can also keep a group of females together if you do not plan to breed them. Keep in mind that female turkeys will still lay eggs with no male present, but the eggs will not be fertile.

Q: *Do heritage turkeys get sick?*

A: Like all animals, heritage turkeys are prone to certain diseases. With proper diet and sanitary practices, however, you can greatly reduce their risk. There are also vaccinations available for certain diseases that your vet may recommend if you live in an area where the risk is high.

Q: *Do I have to incubate heritage turkey eggs?*

A: No, if you do not remove the eggs from the nest then the female turkey will raise them herself. If you want to maximize your egg production for the laying season, however, you will need to remove the eggs and incubate them yourself for hatching.

Q: *Do male heritage turkeys fight?*

A: It is not uncommon for male turkeys to fight, particularly if they do not have enough space to establish their own territory and group of females. It is possible to keep heritage turkeys in large flocks with multiple males but you need to provide enough females that each male has his own group – you will also need plenty of space so the males can keep their groups of females separate.

Q: *What is a poult?*

A: Poult is simply the name given to a baby heritage turkey, though you may be more familiar with the term "chick."

The term poult actually refers to baby birds of all domestic fowl species including pheasants, chickens and ducks.

Q: *Can I keep my turkeys in an open pasture?*

A: An open pasture is the ideal location for a flock of turkeys but you do need to enclosure the pasture with a fence. Fencing is required not only to keep your turkeys in place but also to keep out predators.

Q: *I've heard that it's difficult to raise baby turkeys. Is this true?*

A: The reason many people say it is hard to raise baby turkeys is because it can be tricky to get them used to eating and drinking immediately after they are born. Turkey poults have fairly bad sight after they hatch so you may need to use spotlights to direct them to feeding and watering sites.

Chapter Ten: Relevant Websites

This book provides a wealth of knowledge about keeping and caring for heritage turkeys. Within the pages of this book you should find answers to all of your heritage turkey questions. If you find yourself in need of some additional information, however, this is the right place to look. In this chapter you will find lists of relevant websites regarding heritage turkeys in both the U.S. and the U.K.

1.) Food for Heritage Turkeys

In this chapter you will find links for websites containing information about feeding heritage turkeys. Here you will find resources for buying food, creating a healthy diet and tips for feeding your turkeys.

United States Websites:

"Care and Feeding of Baby Turkeys." Island Seed and Feed. <http://islandseed.com/poultry/turkeys/>

"Feeds and Feeding of Free Range Turkey." American Livestock Breeds Conservancy. <http://www.albc-usa.org/documents/turkeymanual/ALBCturkey-4.pdf>

"Feeding Turkeys." Agricultured. <http://www.agricultured.org/2013/06/13/feeding-turkeys/>

"Feeding Turkeys From Start to Finish." Rooney Feeds Ltd. <http://www.rooneyfeeds.com/NewEquis/poultrys/care%20and%20feeding/instrturkeys.html>

United Kingdom Websites:

"Feeding Turkeys." Small Holder Range.
<http://www.smallholderfeed.co.uk/articles/Feeding-Turkeys.aspx>

"Poultry Feeds." HeyGates.
<http://www.heygatesfeeds.co.uk/general/poultry-feeds/>

"Bagged Organic Turkey Feed." Hi Peak Organic Feeds.
<http://www.hipeak.co.uk/prods/organic_turkey_feed.html

"Organic Turkey Feed." Vitrition Organic Feeds.
<http://www.vitritionorganics.co.uk/productturkey.php>

2.) Care for Heritage Turkeys

In this chapter you will find links for websites containing information about caring for heritage turkeys. Here you will find resources for creating an enclosure, designing a habitat and providing the best care for your turkeys.

United States Websites:

"Turkey Care." FarmSanctuary.org.
<http://www.farmsanctuary.org/wp-content/uploads/2012/06/Animal-Care-Turkeys.pdf>

"Care and Feeding of Baby Turkeys." Island Seed and Feed.
<http://islandseed.com/poultry/turkeys/>

"Turkey Care Sheet." Utah State University Extension.
<http://extension.usu.edu/wasatch/files/uploads/turkey%20care%20sheet.pdf>

"Farm Animal Care – Turkey Care." Farm Animal Shelters.
<http://www.farmanimalshelters.org/care_turkey.htm>

United Kingdom Websites:

Houghton-Wallace, Janice. "Becoming a New Turkey Owner." Smallholder.co.uk.
<http://www.smallholder.co.uk/poultry/1238434.Becoming_a_new_turkey_owner/>

"Turkeys – Key Welfare Issues." The Royal Society for the Prevention of Cruelty to Animals.
<http://www.rspca.org.uk/allaboutanimals/farm/turkeys/keyissues>

"Tips on Raising Turkey Poults." Barling Poultry.
<http://barlingpoultry.co.uk/raisingturkeys.pdf>

"Turkeys on Allotments." The Poultry Guide.
<http://www.ruleworks.co.uk/poultry/domestic-turkeys-bird.asp>

3.) Health Info for Heritage Turkeys

In this chapter you will find links for websites containing information about keeping your heritage turkeys healthy. Here you will find resources about common health problems as well as their symptoms and treatments.

United States Websites:

"Turkey Health Forum." Poultry-Health.com.
<http://www.poultry-health.com/fora/turkhelth/>

"Poultry Health and Management: Chickens, Turkeys, Ducks, Geese and Quail." David Sainsbury.
<http://www.amazon.com/Poultry-Health-Management-Chickens-Turkeys/dp/0632051728>

"Farm Animal Care – Turkey Care." Farm Animal Shelters.
<http://www.farmanimalshelters.org/care_turkey.htm>

"Common Diseases and Ailments of Turkeys and Their Management." American Livestock Breeds Conservancy.
<http://www.albc-usa.org/documents/turkeymanual/ALBCturkey-5.pdf>

"Quick Disease Guide." ThePoultrySite.
<http://www.thepoultrysite.com/diseaseinfo/>

United Kingdom Websites:

"Turkeys." The Chicken Vet.
<http://www.chickenvet.co.uk/health-and-common-diseases/turkeys/index.aspx>

"Poultry Farming: Health Regulations." Gov.uk.
<https://www.gov.uk/poultry-health>

"Turkeys." Crowshall Veterinary Services.
<http://crowshall.co.uk/turkeys.php>

4.) General Info for Heritage Turkeys

In this chapter you will find links for websites containing information about heritage turkeys. Here you will find resources for information about what heritage turkeys are, how they compare to commercial breeds and other general information.

United States Websites:

Niman, Bill and Nicolette Hahn. "Heritage Turkeys: Worth the Cost?" The Atlantic. <http://www.theatlantic.com/health/archive/2010/11/heritage-turkeys-worth-the-cost/66727/>

"Definition of a Heritage Turkey." The American Livestock Breeds Conservation. <http://www.albc-usa.org/cpl/turkdefinition.html>

"Heritage Turkeys." Heritage Turkey Foundation. <http://www.heritageturkeyfoundation.org/>

United Kingdom Websites:

"Heritage Turkeys." HeritageTurkeys.co.uk.
<http://www.heritageturkeys.co.uk/>

"Heritage Turkeys." Raskelf Rare Breeds.
<http://www.raskelfrarebreeds.co.uk/Raskelf_Rare_Breeds/
Heritage_Turkeys.html>

"Organic Turkeys." Rutland Organic Free Range Christmas
Heritage Turkeys.
<http://www.rutlandorganics.co.uk/rutland-heritage-
turkeys.html>

5.) Breeding Heritage Turkeys

In this chapter you will find links for websites containing information about breeding heritage turkeys. Here you will find resources for encouraging your turkeys to breed, setting up a breeding environment and caring for the chicks.

United States Websites:

"Selecting Your Best Turkeys for Breeding." American Livestock Breeds Conservancy. <http://albc-usa.org/ EducationalResources/master_breeder_turkeys.html>

"Turkey Breeding." TNAU Agritech Portal – Animal Husbandry. <http://agritech.tnau.ac.in/animal_husbandry/animhus_tur-breeding.html>

"Raising Heritage Turkeys." Honest Meat. <http://www.honestmeat.com/honest_meat/2008/11/raising-heritage-turkeys-one-farmers-perspective.html>

"Raising Turkeys." ThePoultrySite.
<http://www.thepoultrysite.com/articles/606/raising-turkeys>

"Raising Turkeys at Home." Raising Turkeys Guide.
<http://www.raising-turkeys.com/>

United Kingdom Websites:

"Breeding Heritage Turkeys." HeritageTurkeys.co.uk.
<http://www.heritageturkeys.co.uk/information/breeding.aspx>

"Rutland Organic Breeding Turkeys."
RutlandOrganics.co.uk.
<http://www.rutlandorganics.co.uk/breeding-turkeys.html>

"Breeding." Starting with Turkeys. Published by Broad Leys Publishing Ltd.
<http://www.blpbooks.co.uk/broad_leys_books/start-keeping-turkeys/turkey-breeding-extract.php>

Index

A

American Livestock Breeders Conservancy 12, 55
American Poultry Association.....................3, 14, 17, 18, 20, 21
Animal Welfare Act..25, 124
antibiotics 6, 8, 83, 85, 91
artificial insemination 6, 11, 39, 69
Aspergillosis 81, 82
Auburn 7, 13
Avian Influenza 81, 82

B

babies...67, 68
barn..32, 55, 59, 95
basic information...2
bedding 34, 35, 39, 56, 58, 59, 85, 95
Black................................7, 13, 14, 15, 16, 17, 19, 120, 124
blackhead..81, 83, 84
Bourbon Red 7, 11, 12, 13, 14, 69
breeder 18, 31, 32, 41, 42, 43, 44, 112, 125
breeding.2, 3, 2, 10, 11, 12, 14, 20, 25, 43, 44, 57, 62, 67, 68, 69, 70, 71, 72, 73, 75, 94, 99, 112, 113, 126, 127
breeds 5, 7, 8, 9, 10, 11, 12, 13, 14, 15, 17, 21, 22, 24, 38, 42, 44, 57, 74, 95, 99, 110
brooder..31, 82
Bumblefoot 81, 84

C

care 2, 3, 5, 30, 32, 34, 36, 39, 53, 81, 94, 104, 106, 108, 127

cleaning...56, 58, 59, 73, 89, 96

Coccidiosis...81, 85

color...8, 14, 18, 19, 20, 44, 68

coloration...14, 18, 19, 20, 21, 68

common diseases 81

contamination.. 72

cost 11, 30, 31, 32, 33, 34, 35, 36, 110, 125

costs...23, 30, 33, 34, 35, 36

criteria...6, 13, 69

D

DEFRA 25, 26

Dehydration 81, 86

Department for Environment, Food and Rural Affairs 25, 125

diet............................... 8, 10, 53, 60, 61, 81, 84, 87, 92, 93, 99, 100, 104

diseases...28, 32, 56, 80, 81, 84, 92, 100, 109

E

egg 4, 15, 31, 75, 76, 101

eggs..3, 4, 31, 41, 43, 44, 69, 71, 73, 74, 75, 76, 80, 83, 90, 99, 100, 101, 121

enclosure 3, 25, 28, 30, 32, 34, 55, 57, 78, 84, 87, 102, 106

extinction 2, 12

F

facts 2, 5, 94

Feather Picking 81, 86

feathers........................... 1, 4, 10, 14, 15, 16, 22, 39, 83, 85, 86

fencing 31, 39, 56, 57, 59, 79, 96, 97

fertile 71, 74, 76, 99, 100

flooring..55, 84

food..1, 6, 8, 10, 11, 18, 26, 28, 29, 34, 61, 62, 63, 67, 72, 76, 77, 84, 85, 88, 89, 90, 104, 127

Fowl Cholera 81, 87

frequently asked questions 98

fungus 82

G

genetically-modified 1, 126

Great Britain Poultry Register.............................. 26

growth rate 6, 9, 16, 90, 95, 99

H

habitat..............................2, 53, 54, 58, 94, 106

hatch 41, 76, 90, 102

health..................... 2, 3, 8, 43, 44, 53, 54, 62, 69, 72, 108, 109, 110, 125

healthy 40, 44, 53, 54, 68, 69, 80, 81, 92, 104, 108

Heritage Turkey Foundation..............................12, 110, 125

history 5, 21

humidity..4, 75, 76, 82

I

incubator..75, 76
infection...82, 83, 84, 85, 87, 89, 91
initial cost... 30
insects...10, 18, 34, 62, 91

J

Jersey Buff...7, 13, 14

L

license...23, 24
lifespan..8, 9, 95
lineage... 70

M

mate...6, 69
maturity..18, 61, 63, 64, 96
medicated...29, 84, 90
Midget White..7, 13
monthly costs...30, 34

N

Narragansett...7, 13, 17, 18, 126
nest box...73, 75
nesting boxes.. 35

Newcastle Disease 81, 89

nutritional needs 60

P

pasture...55, 56, 102

Permit 25

pest 10, 39

population...2, 12

poults 31, 35, 41, 43, 44, 61, 63, 64, 71, 76, 77, 78, 82, 83, 86, 88, 96, 102

predators 31, 39, 56, 57, 72, 102

prevention 80, 84, 90

price 10, 30

pros and cons... 38

protein 35, 61, 64, 96, 100

purchasing 2, 23, 31, 36, 44, 80

Q

questions 3, 2, 26, 43, 44, 94, 98, 103, 127

R

raise 2, 27, 28, 39, 75, 101, 102, 127

ratio...27, 61, 69

regulations..24, 25, 26, 125

relevant websites... 103

reproduce 6, 88

Roundworms...81, 90

Royal Palm 7, 12, 13

S

sanitation 25, 29, 83, 84, 89, 90
scientific name...8
size 8, 11, 25, 63, 69, 74
Slate 7, 13, 19, 126
space 25, 27, 38, 39, 54, 62, 69, 77, 86, 87, 93, 101
standard...1, 10, 14, 17, 18, 68
Standard Bronze 7, 10, 13, 17, 18, 20
symptoms 81, 83, 85, 89, 90, 108

T

temperature 75, 76
treatment.................................. 26, 36, 80, 81, 83, 84, 85, 88, 89, 90, 91
turkey feed...35, 61, 63
Turkey Pox 81, 91

V

vaccinate..29, 33, 92
veterinarian 41, 93
veterinary...30, 32, 34, 36, 39

W

water....................... 28, 32, 59, 60, 64, 76, 77, 78, 86, 87, 89, 91, 93, 96
weight 11, 17, 64, 90

White Holland 7, 13, 21, 22, 126

wild birds 26, 28, 32, 56, 62, 72, 83, 88

wild turkeys 6, 8, 15, 20, 24

Photo Credits

Title Page Photo By Curt Gibbs from Long Beach, California (Heritage Turkeys) [CC-BY-2.0 (http://creativecommons.org/licenses/by/2.0)], via Wikimedia Commons, <http://commons.wikimedia.org/wiki/File:Heritage_Turkeys_in_MD.jpg>

Page 1 Photo By Flickr user Charlie Day Daytime Studios, <http://www.flickr.com/photos/60700203@N03/8159454095/sizes/l/>

Page 5 Photo By Hatmatbbat10 via Wikimedia Commons, <http://en.wikipedia.org/wiki/File:Turkeybird.JPG>

Page 11 Photo By Mtshad via Wikimedia Commons, <http://en.wikipedia.org/wiki/File:Bourbob_red_turkey_Tom-r2.jpg>

Page 16 Photo By Hunter Desportes via Wikimedia Commons, <http://en.wikipedia.org/wiki/File:Black_Spanish_toms_and_hen.jpg>

Page 23 Photo By Steven Walling via Wikimedia Commons, <http://en.wikipedia.org/wiki/File:Beltsville_Small_White.jpg>

Page 26 Photo By Flickr user Stevevoght, <http://www.flickr.com/photos/voght/2441818832/sizes/l/>

Page 40 Photo By Matt Billings via Wikimedia Commons, <http://en.wikipedia.org/wiki/File:Bourbon_Red_tom_close-up.jpg>

Page 43 Photo By Flickr user Lee Edwin Coursey, <http://www.flickr.com/photos/leeco/31533181/sizes/o/>

Page 53 Photo By Riki7 via Wikimedia Commons, <http://en.wikipedia.org/wiki/File:Gall-dindi.jpg>

Page 54 Photo By James Emery from Douglasville, United States (Turkey_2689) [CC-BY-2.0 (http://creativecommons.org/licenses/by/2.0)], via Wikimedia Commons, <http://commons.wikimedia.org/wiki/File:Bourbon_Red_turkeys.jpg>

Page 60 Photo By Flickr user HeyPaul, <http://www.flickr.com/photos/heypaul/2449650/sizes/l/>

Page 67 Photo By Kristie Gianopulus via Wikimedia Commons,
<http://en.wikipedia.org/wiki/File:Baby_turkey_in_FL.jpg>

Page 68 Photo By Justin Piper (Own work) [Public domain], via Wikimedia Commons,
<http://commons.wikimedia.org/wiki/File:Bourbon_Red_Turkey.JPG>

Page 71 Photo By D. Gordon E. Robertson via Wikimedia Commons,
<http://en.wikipedia.org/wiki/File:Wild_Turkey_nest_and_eggs.jpg>

Page 74 Photo By D. Gordon E. Robertson via Wikimedia Commons,
<http://en.wikipedia.org/wiki/File:Wild_turkey_and_juveniles.jpg>

Page 77 Photo By Mtshad via Wikimedia Commons,
<http://en.wikipedia.org/wiki/File:Bourbon-Red-Turkey-Poult.jpg>

Page 80 Photo by Shakeelgilgity, via Wikimedia Commons, <http://en.wikipedia.org/wiki/File:Domestic_turkey_in_Pakistan.jpg>

Page 92 Photo By Flickr user Clevergrrl, <http://www.flickr.com/photos/clevergrrl/3211275957/sizes/o/>

Page 94 Photo By Flickr user Luagh45, <http://www.flickr.com/photos/luagh45/6423069819/sizes/o/>

Page 98 Photo By Flickr user Valeehill, <http://www.flickr.com/photos/valeehill/2782138194/sizes/o/>

Page 103 Photo By Flickr user Valeehill, <http://www.flickr.com/photos/valeehill/2782137738/sizes/o/>

References

"Animal Welfare Act 2006." Legislation.gov.uk.
<http://www.legislation.gov.uk/ukpga/2006/45/contents>

"Black Turkey." The American Livestock Breeds
Conservancy. < http://www.albc-usa.org/cpl/black.html>

"Bronze Turkey." The American Livestock Breeds
Conservancy. < http://www.albc-usa.org/cpl/bronze.html>

"Buff Turkey." The American Livestock Breeds
Conservancy. < http://www.albc-usa.org/cpl/buff.html>

"Common Diseases and Ailments of Turkeys and Their
Management." American Livestock Breeds Conservancy.
<http://www.albc-
usa.org/documents/turkeymanual/ALBCturkey-5.pdf>

"Definition of a Heritage Turkey." The American Livestock
Breeds Conservation. <http://www.albc-
usa.org/cpl/turkdefinition.html>

"Economics of Heritage Turkey Production." The American
Livestock Breeds Conservancy – How to Raise Heritage

Turkeys On Pasture. <http://www.albc-usa.org/documents/turkeymanual/ALBCturkey-13.pdf>

"Glossary of Poultry Terms." University of Kentucky College of Agriculture, Food and Environment. <http://afspoultry.ca.uky.edu/extension-glossary>

"Heritage Turkeys." Heritage Turkey Foundation. <http://www.heritageturkeyfoundation.org/>

Niman, Bill and Nicolette Hahn. "Heritage Turkeys: Worth the Cost?" The Atlantic. <http://www.theatlantic.com/health/archive/2010/11/heritage-turkeys-worth-the-cost/66727/>

"Poultry Farms: General Regulations." Department for Environment, Food and Rural Affairs. <https://www.gov.uk/poultry-farms-general-regulations>

"Quick Disease Guide." ThePoultrySite. <http://www.thepoultrysite.com/diseaseinfo/>

"Selecting Your Best Turkeys for Breeding." American Livestock Breeds Conservancy. <http://albc-usa.org/EducationalResources/master_breeder_turkeys.html>

"Slate Turkey." The American Livestock Breeds Conservancy. < http://www.albc-usa.org/cpl/slate.html>

"Turkey Breeding." TNAU Agritech Portal – Animal Husbandry. <http://agritech.tnau.ac.in/animal_husbandry/animhus_tur-breeding.html>

"Turkey Talk: Broad-Breasted Whites vs. Heritage Turkeys." How Stuff Works. <http://science.howstuffworks.com/life/genetic/genetically-modified-turkey1.htm>

"Turkeys – Key Welfare Issues." The Royal Society for the Prevention of Cruelty to Animals. <http://www.rspca.org.uk/allaboutanimals/farm/turkeys/keyissues>

"Turkeys: Narragansett." The American Livestock Breeds Conservancy. < http://www.albc-usa.org/cpl/narragansett.html>

"White Holland Turkey." The American Livestock Breeds Conservancy. < http://www.albc-usa.org/cpl/wholland.html>
